THE BOY

WHO TURNED

LIVES AROUND

AS THE WORLD

TURNED UPSIDE DOWN!

无畏世界危机的小救星

Author: Celene Ting
作者：陈欣桐

Illustrator: Tommy Wong
绘图：王位义

To order additional copies of this book, contact
Toll Free +65 3165 7531 (Singapore)
Toll Free +60 3 3099 4412 (Malaysia)
www.partridgepublishing.com/singapore
orders.singapore@partridgepublishing.com

ISBN
978-1-5437-6311-9 (sc)
978-1-5437-6313-3 (hc)
978-1-5437-6312-6 (e)

Print information available on the last page.

06/14/2021

PARTRIDGE

THE BOY WHO TURNED LIVES AROUND AS THE WORLD TURNED UPSIDE DOWN!

无畏世界危机的小救星

Author: Celene Ting
Illustrator: Tommy Wong
Book Design: Lilly Han
Art Direction & Layout: John Lim

Dedication
献词

This book is dedicated to my beloved son, Tommy, who (still) thinks I am "the most magical Mommy in the world"; my amazing niece, Beatrice and awesome nephew, Keivian; Aunty Dina, family and friends for riding out life's storms with us.

这本书特别献给我最爱的儿子位义，一个(依然)将我当成他心目中"神奇妈咪"的小宝贝、亲爱的恩慈(侄女)和明凯(侄儿)、也非常感谢一路以来支持我们的家人、家里的一份子Dina阿姨以及与我们一起走过风风雨雨的好朋友。

Special thanks to my brother, Desmond, who helps and supports me in everything I do (including fixing this story).

我也要特别谢谢我的弟弟文彪，他总在我最需要帮助的时候第一个站出来，用心地陪伴、鼓励和助我一臂之力(包括修改这本书的内容)。

To Johnny, I am always grateful to you for being a loving and engaged father to our son.

还有谢谢德耀，一直在背后默默支持和疼惜我们的儿子位义，他对孩子所付出的爱不曾少过。

And, to God for setting His rainbow in the clouds to remind us that His promises are true.

在此也感谢上帝总在风雨后，为我们在天空画出漂亮的彩虹。是上帝让我们知道无论处于任何困境，也无需感到绝望，因为祂一直与我们同在。

Genesis 9: 13-16

创世纪 9: 13-16

Once upon a time, there was a boy named Tommy who lived happily with his parents in a house with a *neat, little rooftop garden.*

很久以前，有个可爱独立的小男孩名叫位义，他和爸爸妈妈快乐地住在一起。他们家的**天台有一个小小的色彩花园**，里面种满了红绿色的新鲜蔬果和美丽的花朵。

Tommy loved the *flowers, fruits and vegetables* that he helped his mother to grow. Every day, he cared for them tirelessly — *rain or shine.*

位义非常爱护他亲手帮妈妈栽种的**蔬果和花朵。**不管任何天气或心情，他每天都**风雨不改**地上天台照顾那些花花草草。

As the years went by, however, *climate change* took a toll on their way of life.

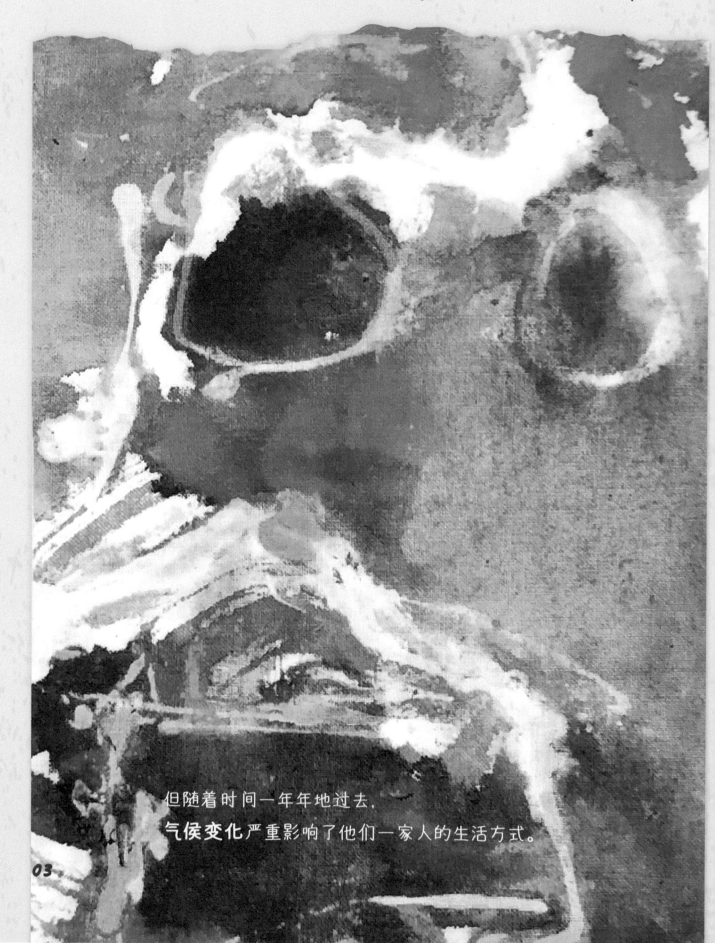

但随着时间一年年地过去，
气侯变化严重影响了他们一家人的生活方式。

It became a constant challenge to predict and to prepare for the changes brought about by *extreme weather conditions.*

现在的天气就像魔术一样，分分秒秒都在变幻。**极端无常的气候所带**来的变化，简直今人捉摸不清，措不及防。

During *downpours, flooding* occurred in the streets and in the family's rooftop garden.

每当**倾盆大雨**，位义家外面的街道和天台上的小花园经常会被雨水**淹没**。

Tommy's mother would rush to the rooftop to *shelter and shield* their beautiful blooms for fear they would be crushed by *strong winds and heavy rain*.

位义的妈妈这时会撑着多把小雨伞，冲到天台为刚盛开的花草**遮风挡雨**，否则它们将被**暴风雨**吹歪压弯，掉落在地上。

On *scorching hot* days, Tommy could fry an egg easily in his rooftop garden as it sat sizzling in his little cooking pan.

在**暴晒的天气**时，位义会在天台上用自己的迷你平底锅煎太阳蛋。

This was possible with just a *solar stove*, thanks to plenty of light and heat on such sunny days!

就算没有煤气，位义也可以使用**太阳能炉**把一颗颗蛋煎得"滋滋"作响！

And, as Tommy played in the sweltering heat, his mother would head upstairs *hurriedly* to dry the wet laundry before the rain came again.

正当位义玩得汗流浃背时，妈妈便会**急忙**
冲上天台，趁暴风雨来临之前把湿衣服晾干。

09

Seeing the abundance of light and rain, Tommy decided to embark on an exciting journey to seek out new and creative ways to *harness the sun and rain*... right in his very own backyard!

只要位义看到充足的阳光或雨水，他精灵的小脑袋就不停转呀转，并思考该如何好好**善用天然资源**，在家里的后院创造一些崭新和有趣的玩意儿！

Tommy pondered over how he could use *solar and hydroelectric energy* to power up his father's electric car.

位义突然想到，他可以善用太阳公公和雨婆婆的能量（太阳能和水能）来启动爸爸的电动车。

The need to re-charge his father's electric car was inconvenient at times.

During traffic congestions, it was tough to find a *public charging station for electric vehicles.*

爸爸的电动车偶尔会出点小状况，尤其是塞车时恰巧没电，而周围却找不到任何**电动汽车公共充电站**。

After a quick scan of his home, Tommy found things he could *recycle or reuse* for his exciting endeavour!

想到这点，位义迅速地环顾家里的四周。不一会儿，他找到一些可以拿来**循环或重复使用**的物件和材料！

They included *used water and shower pipes* as well as other construction tools that Tommy dug out from his father's shed.

这些物件包括了**旧水管**、**沐浴软管**和其他建筑工具，都是位义从爸爸的工具储藏室里挖出来的。

Using connecting pipes of various lengths and sizes, Tommy created a *mobile water wall* that he later attached to a network of dynamos.

位义一开始先把不同长度和尺寸的水管接驳起来，然后成功造出一座连接着发电系统的**移动式水墙**。

Tommy and his father then tried to make *water wheels* out of *stainless steel* and other *composite materials* that they found in the garage.

位义和爸爸接着尝试把他们在车库里找到的**不锈钢**材料，以及其他**复合材料**凑起来改造成**水轮**。

Whenever it poured, rainwater gushing through the pipes caused the wheels to spin and drive the *generator*, thus, producing *hydroelectricity*.

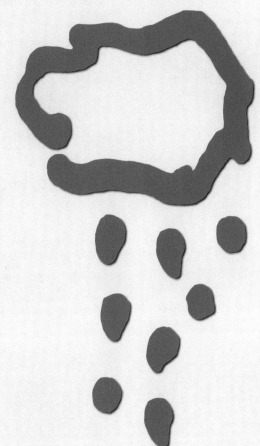

所以只要下起大雨，天空倒下来的雨水就会"哗啦啦"地流入水管并使轮子转动，从而启动**发电机**生产水电能。

Thereafter, they attached this *unique system* to their electric car. They were thrilled to see that their extraordinary setup could power up the electric car even if the latter's battery became depleted!

之后，他们父子俩发现这个**奇特的系统**，即使在没有电池的情况下也可以发动他们的电动车呢！

But, wait, there's more!
等一等，接下来还有更精彩的！

Tommy and his father also added *solar panels*, cameras, sensors and other aerodynamic features to their electric car. Now, their family car could be powered up by converting the sun's rays into *electrical energy* as well.

位义和爸爸还在电动车装上一片片的**太阳能板**，将太阳能转化为**电能**。然后，他们也装了监控摄像机、感应器和各种空气动力性能，使电动车在太阳高挂时开起来更稳也更有劲。

To tap on the frequent *gusts and gales* in their neighbourhood, they developed a miniature *wind turbine*. To that end, they pieced together flattened tin cans and aluminium sheets.

为了充分利用屋子外面常有的**狂风**，他们用扁平的铝罐和铝板，合力制造出一台迷你**风力发电机**。

Using waste crate boxes, they sawed *plastic, propeller-like vanes*. These turned around a rotor that was connected to the main shaft which spun the generator to produce electricity.

他们同时把收纳箱里的**塑料**，锯成几个**旋螺浆叶片**围着转子绕转，再接到转动发电机的主轴上就成功发电了。

Spinning freely in the wind, the small wind turbine not only helped to supply electricity but also doubled up as *propellers* for the electric car.

这台小型风力发电机不但能自由运转，为电动车供应电力，它同时也充作发动电动车的**旋螺浆叶片**。

Finally, they equipped their car with a *remote control console*. This enabled Tommy to navigate his family's *hybrid electric car* without the need to drive it himself!

最后，他们一家人还设计一个**远程遥控器**。这样一来，位义只需按几颗钮就能在无人驾驶的情况下，随意遥控一手改造的**混合动力汽车**了！

Now, their family car could take off by air or by land - *rain or shine* - anytime, anywhere!

转眼间，他们的家庭汽车已设置了陆空兼备，**不惧风雨**，随时随地开动的功能啦！

Their sense of imagination injected a *new lease of life* and revealed magical wonders in every corner of their home... and, neighbourhood.

位义一家人的突发奇想为屋内和社区里的每个角落注入了**新生机**，为此开展了奇妙的契机。

Soon, word about the *ingenuity* of Tommy's family got around town. People from near and far approached them with some strange and incredible ideas.

没多久，位义一家人**机智灵巧的点子**很快传遍了整个社区。远远近近的人都跑来找位义和他父母，还与他们分享各种奇奇怪怪的有趣点子。

Among these was a *pushcart with 'wings'* that could house and transport medicines, food and groceries by air or by land.

其中一个非常有意义的点子是改造一部'**机翼**'滑轮推车，以空运或陆运的方式来帮助每户家庭运送生活必需品，例如:药物、食物和干粮杂货，等等。

This, Tommy thought, would be a *game changer*. Seniors or persons with special needs could have essential supplies delivered to their doorstep without the need to step out of their homes at all!

位义觉得这项发明**颠覆了传统的购物模式**，尤其是让年长者及有特殊需要的人士在无需出门的情况下，快速方便地获取他们所需的日常用品了！

Adopting *one-of-a-kind* and do-it-yourself designs, Tommy and his parents built an **amazing pushcart** for their elder neighbour, Mrs Poh-Jo, who lived alone.

位义和爸爸妈妈因此马上动工，全家齐心合力造出一部**外形独特**、手工制作的**神奇推车**，送给他们较年长又独居的邻居，Poh-Jo老太太。

To construct Mrs Poh-Jo's pushcart, they first put together unwanted *styrofoam boxes* and wheels of abandoned toys that they found in their estate's rubbish chute.

他们连忙把在院子垃圾槽里找到的废弃**保丽龙盒**和玩具轮子，拿来筑成Poh-Jo老太太的推车。

After creating and connecting *wooden wings* to Mrs Poh-Jo's remote-controlled pushcart, Tommy and his parents taught her how to manoeuvre and fly it.

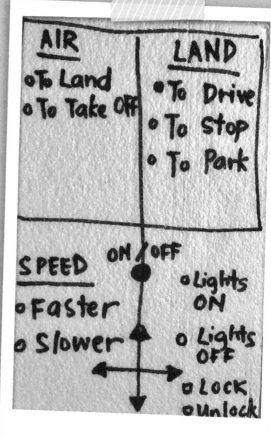

位义和爸爸妈妈在Poh-Jo老太太的推车装上**轻木机翼**后，再详细地教她如何巧妙地操作远程遥控器，让推车飞起来。

Similar to their modified, *hybrid electric car*, Mrs Poh-Jo's *customised cart* could be powered by *hydroelectric, solar or wind energy* - with or without batteries - in *all* weather conditions!

这部为Poh-Jo老太太**量身定做的推车**，跟他们之前改造的**混合动力汽车**几乎一样，无论天气如何，它都可以在有或无电池情况下，靠水力、风力发电或太阳能自动操作！

The family's *life-saving invention* proved extremely useful during peacetime and disasters of all kinds, even during a *pandemic* when it was difficult or dangerous for folks like Mrs Poh-Jo to leave their homes.

无论在日常生活中或灾难时期，位义一家人的**救生发明**发挥了最大的功效，帮助了许多人。尤其在**大流行疫情**当下，像Poh-Jo老太太一样不方便出门的年长者，都认为它是一种必不可少的好工具。

From the comfort of their homes, people could now *navigate* their **souped-up carts** with wheels and wings to fetch and deliver anything... rain or shine!

从此以后，大家可以舒服地坐在家里一手**引航**装有机翼和滑轮的**加强版推车**，不惧风雨地四处载送货物，真是方便又安全！

Not only did Tommy and his family's inventions open the doors to many *new opportunities*, they also helped *turn lives around* even as the world seemed to turn upside down!

位义一家人的发明不但打开了许多**机会之门**，也帮助其他人**从艰苦的生活中站了起来**，使他们更勇敢地面对和战胜世界危机！

With Love,
Tommy Wong & Family
王位义和家人

36

作者语录

这个故事的创作灵感取自于2020年发生的真实事件。当时新加坡政府首度宣布推行一系列社区缓解措施，以遏制导致全球COVID-19新型冠状病毒大流行的SARS-CoV-2（严重急性呼吸综合征冠状病毒2）在当地扩散和跨境传播。

那时我们顿觉被困在家里封闭的四面墙内，身边只剩下手机和电脑等设备。我们一家唯有尝试在"新常态"环境下工作、玩乐和学习新事物。即便如此，我们不想被疫情打败，所以在自家天台上展开了一段难忘有趣的探索之旅，成功研创出崭新、独特及伸缩性强的神奇工具！

一年过去了，我们又回到了原点。当我在下笔写作时，新加坡正极力应对由变异新冠病毒在社区内爆发的新一波感染疫情。因此，我希望这本书能够成为黑暗中的一点光，向我们当中的英雄（包括所有医护人员、外籍劳工和必要工作者）、家人和朋友致谢。谢谢您与我们共同携手抗疫，在经历本世纪最艰难的时刻依然彼此守望。

当有天我们回顾时，希望大家记得即使COVID-19新型冠状病毒在彼此之间筑起了一堵无形的墙，但我们依然凭着信心和盼望持续付出、祝福别人和感恩所拥有的平安。

Author's Notes

This story was inspired by true events that took place in Singapore when community mitigation measures were first announced in 2020 to curb local and cross-border transmission of the novel coronavirus, SARS-CoV-2, that caused the worldwide COVID-19 pandemic.

Back then, we found ourselves confined within the four walls of our home. Left to our own devices, our family attempted to adjust to a 'new normal' way of working, playing and learning from home. Refusing to be defeated, we embarked on an unforgettable journey of discovery that revealed a realm of restoration, renewal and resilience... right in our very own rooftop!

A year on, it appears we are back to where we started. At the time of writing, Singapore is battling a new wave of infections in the community caused by emerging virus variants.

Therefore, I hope this book serves as the light that shines out of the darkness before us. I wish to dedicate it to the heroes in our midst (including all healthcare, migrant and essential workers), family and friends who forged memorable bonds with us during the crucible of the most challenging crisis of this century.

When we look back some day, may we be humbled and heartened to know that even as the COVID-19 pandemic erected walls between us, we rose above it by faith and with hope, always giving our best while giving thanks.

Lightning Source UK Ltd.
Milton Keynes UK
UKHW050026220621
385933UK00002B/100